Lieve Baeten

The Curious Little Witch

NorthSouth
New York / London

It was a bright, moonlit night, and the whole world was sleeping. But in one house, the lights were still shining.

Lizzy and her cat were flying on their broomstick when
they spotted it.

Being a curious little witch, Lizzy flew down to the house
and peered through the open window. And what did she see?

Mice! Cat leaped off the broomstick, knocking Lizzy
right through the open window. The little witch landed
with a clatter. And worse still, her broomstick broke!

What a disaster! She couldn't fly home on a broken
broomstick! But what was that she heard? Music?

Being a curious little witch, Lizzy crept down the
stairs to have a closer look.

"Hello," said Lizzy. "What lovely music you make."
"Of course it's lovely music," said the Music Witch.
"I'm the witch who makes music. And who might you be?"

"I'm Lizzy," said Lizzy. "My broomstick broke when
I fell through your window. Can you fix it?"

"I can't fix broomsticks, I'm afraid," said the Music
Witch. "I only know about music."

The Music Witch's music was sublime.
But what was that wonderful smell?

Mmmmmm. Being a curious little witch, Lizzy
decided to follow her nose.

"Hello," said Lizzy. "Something down here smells delicious."

"Of course it smells delicious," said the Kitchen Witch. "I'm the witch who knows how to cook. And who might you be?"

"I'm Lizzy," said Lizzy. "My broomstick broke when I fell through your window. Can you fix it?"

"I can't fix broomsticks, I'm afraid," said the Kitchen Witch. "I only know about cooking. Are you hungry, by any chance?"

The Kitchen Witch was a wonderful cook. "That was delicious!" said Lizzy, licking her fingers. "Now let me try to magic something for *you* to eat."

"Eeeeeeeek!" shrieked the Kitchen Witch. "Spinach with grasshoppers! How disgusting!"

Lizzy thought she had better leave quickly. She headed down the stairs.

"Hello," said Lizzy. "What a cozy bed you have."

"Of course I have a cozy bed," said the Bedroom Witch. "I am the witch who can magic you to sleep. And who might you be?"

"I'm Lizzy," said Lizzy. "My broomstick broke
when I fell through your window. Can you fix it?"
"I can't fix broomsticks, I'm afraid," said the
Bedroom Witch. "But I can put it to sleep if you like."

"Oh, we don't have time for sleep," said Lizzy,
and she crept down the stairs on tiptoe.

Lizzy found herself in the basement. "Hello," she said.
"Who are you?"

"I'm the witch who likes to tinker with things," said
the Tinkering Witch. "And who might you be?"

"I'm Lizzy," said Lizzy. "My broomstick broke
when I fell through your window. Can you fix it?"

"Of course I can!" said the Tinkering Witch. "I can
fix anything!"

In the blink of an eye, the Tinkering Witch conjured up a
brand-new broomstick for Lizzy, a special rocket-powered
broomstick.

Lizzy gasped. "Now, that really IS magic!"

With a roar, Lizzy dashed out into the night on her
brand-new, rocket-powered broomstick. And what did she see?

Another house with a light still shining . . . !

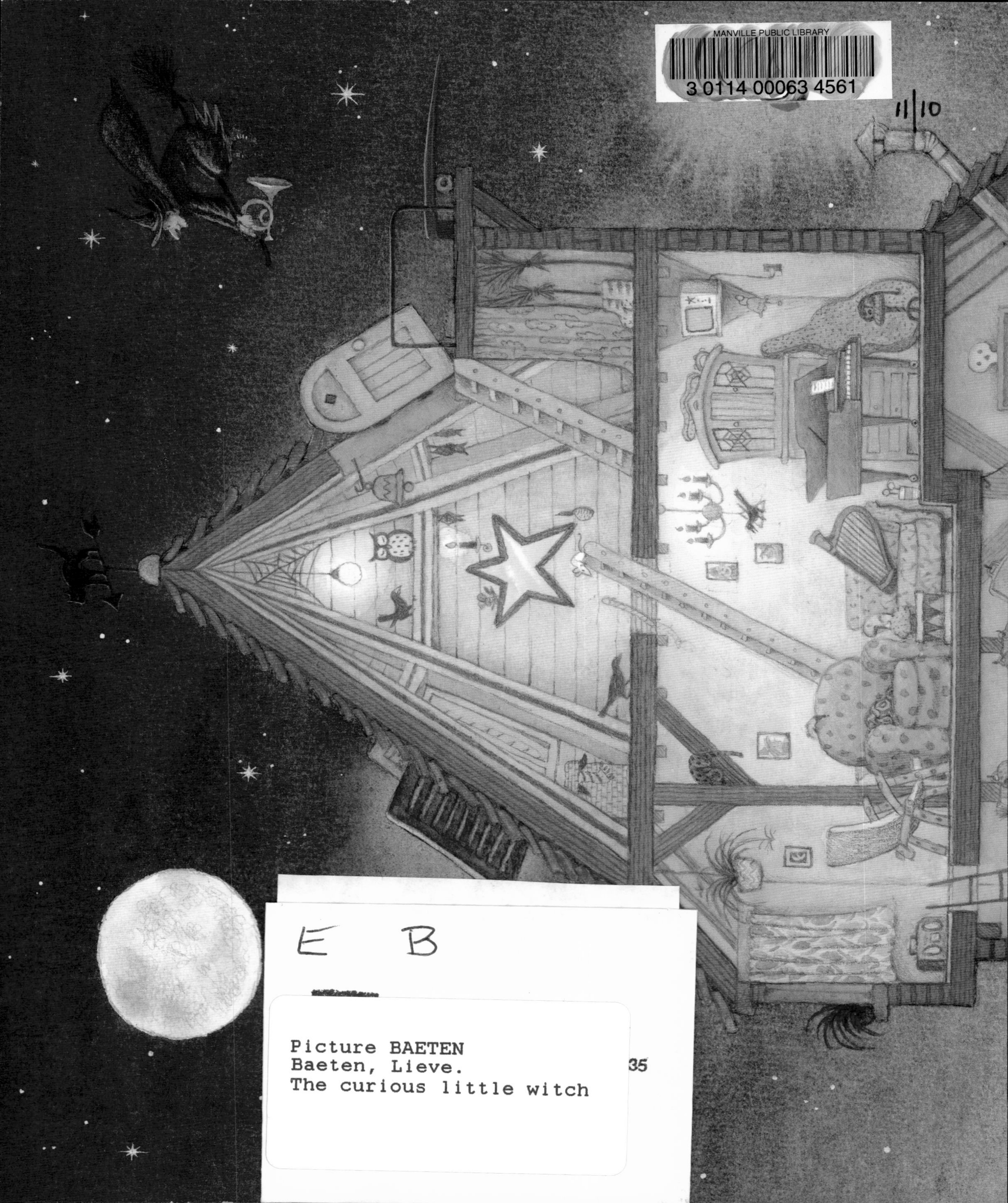